For Ava and Pepé

FLOOF

Heidi McKinnon

Algonquin Young Readers   2024

Floof is floofy.

Floof is **very** floofy.

Floof is the floofiest!

Good morning, Floof.

Floof meows.

Floof eats.

Floof is ready for a busy day.

Floof reads.

Floof gardens.

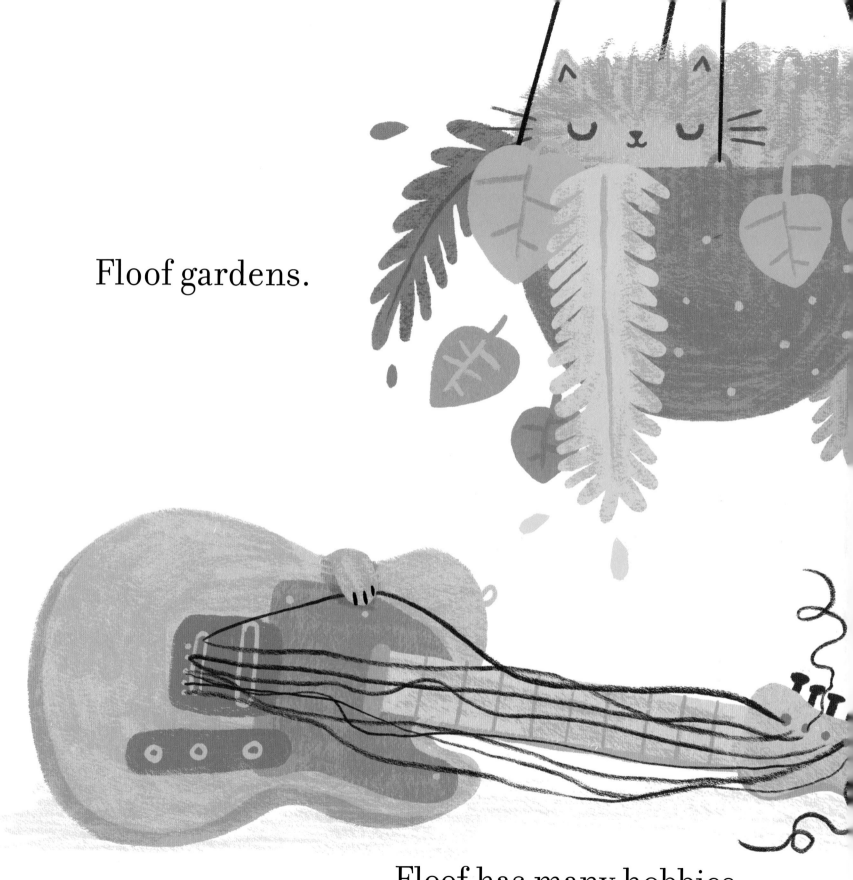

Floof has many hobbies.

Floof fits.

Floof sits.

Floof can disappear.

Floof has important work to do.

Very important

work

to do.

Floof has friends.

Floof has **lots** of friends.

This is **not** Floof's friend.

Floof does not care.

Floof has better things to do.

Floof meows.

Floof eats.

Floof has had a busy day.

Time for bed, Floof.

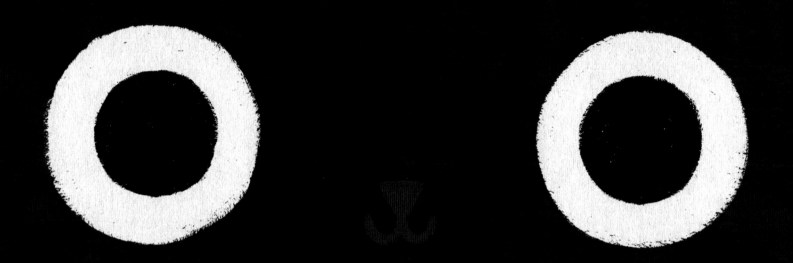

Lights out.

Sleep tight.

Tomorrow will be another busy day.

Published by Algonquin Young Readers
an imprint of Workman Publishing Co., Inc.
a subsidiary of Hachette Book Group, Inc.
1290 Avenue of the Americas
New York, New York 10104

Library of Congress Cataloging-in-Publication Data has been applied for.

ISBN 978-1-5235-2586-7 (hardcover)

Printed in China. Cover and text design by Heidi McKinnon.

10 9 8 7 6 5 4 3 2 1
First US Edition